The Ice-Cream Factory

Contents

Annie Ortiz

Photographed by Anthony Hart

Rigby

Our Field Trip

Do you ever wonder how some things are made? Our class wondered about ice cream, our favorite dessert. So we took a tour through an ice-cream factory and found out!

These tanks hold 40,000 gallons each!

Great big trucks bring milk from dairy farms to the factory. Workers pump the milk into big tanks.

Mixing Machines

The first machine heats the milk to kill any germs. We didn't know milk had germs! Then another machine mixes the heated milk until it's smooth.

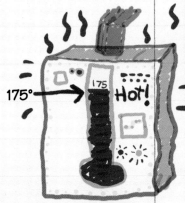

175° Hot!

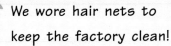

We wore hair nets to keep the factory clean!

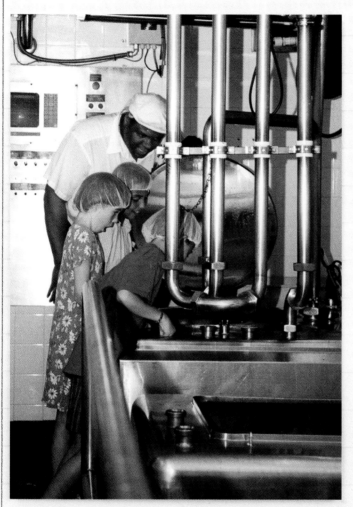

The milk then goes into a blender like the ones we have at home—only much bigger! The blender is run by a computer.

Ingredients

2,300 pounds of sugar are in one bag. They use 10 to 12 bags each day.

Other Ingredients Can Include

eggs

fruit

nuts

The blender mixes cream and sugar with the milk. Our mouths are starting to water!

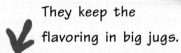
They keep the flavoring in big jugs.

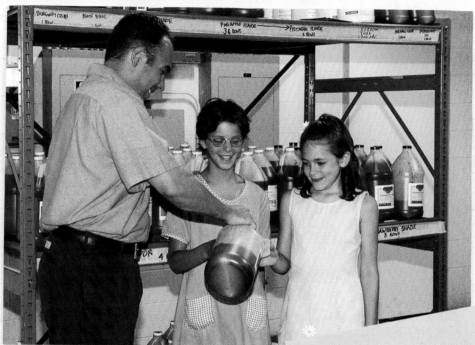

The factory makes two flavors of ice cream each day. Workers cut up fruit, like strawberries and peaches, to add to the ice cream.

Regular Flavors

Homemade Vanilla

Buttered Pecan

Milk Chocolate

Peppermint

Freezing

Then the ice cream goes through freezing pipes. The pipes are so cold that ice forms on them.

ice - 20 degrees

Do not touch.

That makes the ice cream cold and soft. Yum!

Packing

Wear earplugs. Too much noise.

Fruit Flavors

Banana Split

Strawberry

Peaches & Vanilla

Cherry Vanilla

Lemon

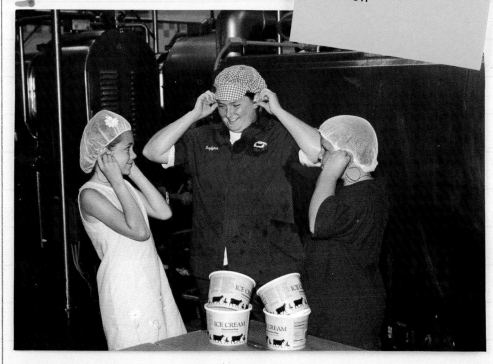

In the packing area, the machines are very fast and VERY noisy. The workers have to wear earplugs. We had to wear earplugs, too!

Watching the machines was fun. One squirts the ice cream into cartons. Another spins the cartons around and around to get rid of air bubbles.

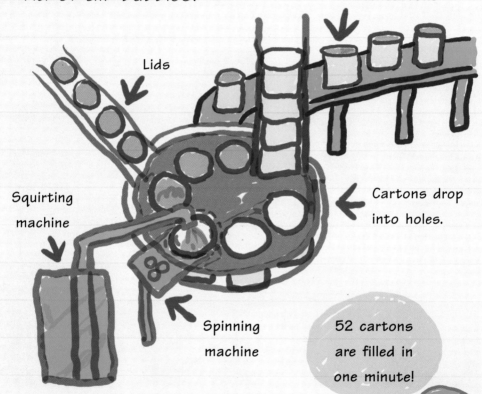

Filled cartons

Lids

Squirting machine

Cartons drop into holes.

Spinning machine

52 cartons are filled in one minute!

10

Hard Freezing

Finally, the ice cream is frozen solid in a very, very cold room. There is a machine that moves the air around. It is so cold it feels like 100° below zero in that room!

Cookie Flavors

Chocolate Chip

Cookies and Cream

Chocolate Chip Cookie Dough

Fudge Brownie Nut

Hot Fudge Brownie

Unusual Flavors

Rocky Road

S'mores

Tin Roof

Peanut Butter Cup

It is so cold that the workers
need to leave the freezer every 20 minutes
to warm up. They can't wear contacts
because they would freeze to their eyes!

Yuck! That's cold!

Shipping

Big trucks take the ice cream to stores. The trucks are like big freezers on wheels.

13

Flowchart

1: Trucks bring milk to big tanks.

8: Trucks take ice cream to stores.

2: Milk is heated and made smooth.

3: Cream and sugar are added and stirred.

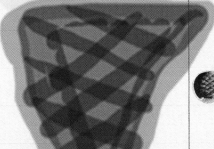

7: It's frozen solid in a cold blast room.

6: It is put in cartons.

4: Flavors are added.

5: The ice cream goes through freezing pipes.

15

Survey

We took a survey of our favorite flavors. We're hungry!

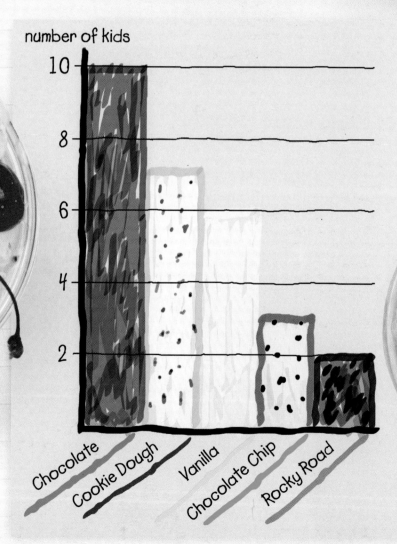

number of kids

Chocolate · Cookie Dough · Vanilla · Chocolate Chip · Rocky Road